Sir Deedrick and his
Delightfully Dauntless Dogs of Delicious Dynamics

for Ruth

Commendably Concise Collection of Convenient Congressional Cataloging

First Aladdin Paperbacks edition October 1996
Copyright © 1990 by Lisa Campbell Ernst
Aladdin Paperbacks
An imprint of Simon & Schuster
Children's Publishing Division
1230 Avenue of the Americas, New York, NY 10020
All rights reserved, including the right of reproduction in whole or in part
in any form
Also available in an Atheneum Books for Young Readers edition.
Printed and bound in Hong Kong
10 9 8 7 6 5 4 3 2 1
The Library of Congress has cataloged the hardcover edition as follows:
Ernst, Lisa Campbell. Ginger jumps/By Lisa
Campbell Ernst.—1st ed. p. cm.
Summary: Ginger the dog loves performing
in the circus, but she is unable to summon
the courage for a new trick until she
finds the little girl companion about whom
she has been dreaming.
ISBN 0-02-733565-8
[1. Dogs—Fiction.   2. Circus—Fiction.]
1. Title. PZ7.E7323Gi
1990 [E]—dc20   89-38706
ISBN 0-689-80652-3 (Aladdin pbk.)

GINGER
JUMPS

Lisa Campbell Ernst

Aladdin Paperbacks

For as long as Ginger could remember, the circus had been her home. She grew up with the elephants, camels, and horses. She knew all of the clowns, acrobats, and aerialists.

It was an exciting life, but every day from dawn to dusk, the circus seemed to rush past her: Tents were set up, acts practiced, and shows performed. Then down came the tents, and the circus moved on to the next town.

No one had time to play with a small, brown puppy.

When she was little, Ginger often watched the dogs who were old enough to perform. They practiced each day with Sir Deedrick, "The Duke of Dogs." Teaching so many dogs new tricks kept Sir Deedrick terribly busy. "Cocoa, Tippy, Buster! Hot Dog, Taffy, Peaches! Speedy, Gretchen, Prunella!"

In the show, Prunella was the main attraction. She always wore the fanciest costumes and got the most biscuit treats. "I'm the best," she gloated.

Day after day, Ginger looked on, hoping that someone might stop to play. But Sir Deedrick and his daredevil dogs had more important things to do.

As Ginger grew older, Sir Dee-drick taught her simple circus tricks, like walking on her hind legs and jumping through hoops. She paid close attention to his instructions and learned to do each trick precisely right. With time, Ginger was fitted for her fancy collar and joined the other dogs in the ring.

One day as Ginger practiced her two-legged walk, Prunella sauntered over. "No need to try so hard," she sneered. "The people clap only for me, the star of the show — not for a runty dog like you."

Ginger was so surprised that she didn't know what to say. Instead she stretched up taller and bal-anced on *one* leg.

Gradually Ginger became more expert at her new tricks and less nervous about dropping the ball or falling down. Now she began to notice the audience. Clearly, everyone loved Sir Deedrick's dog show. But the ones who clapped the longest and cheered the loudest were the children.

"Sniveling brats," Prunella called them, munching on a biscuit treat. Ginger disagreed. She loved how the children watched, spellbound, on the edge of their seats; how they waved and laughed and jumped up, spilling their popcorn and peanuts.

For Ginger, the children were more fascinating than the circus acts, and each night she ran to the edge of the stands to watch the crowd. The children made her happy.

Even after the crowds were gone, Ginger thought about the children and wondered what they were doing. She had heard stories about dogs that lived with children and their families. What a life!

"I wish I had a real family," she whispered to herself, "with a little girl who had time to play with someone who loves her."

So began Ginger's dreams about the little girl. Sometimes her hair was brown, other times black, or red. Sometimes she liked hot dogs, and in other dreams peanuts were her favorite food. Always, though, the little girl was happy.

Awaking, Ginger often heard the sound of laughter echoing in the air.

One morning, Ginger's dream of the night before seemed so real that she could almost feel the little girl's arms around her.

"I must find her," Ginger whispered. But how? Ginger knew in an instant. Didn't the circus travel from town to town? It's only a matter of time, she told herself, before my little girl walks through the tent door.

She began her search that very night. Standing at the circus entrance, Ginger watched each child who entered the tent, and listened to every laugh. So many faces and so many voices. But none belonged to the girl of Ginger's dreams.

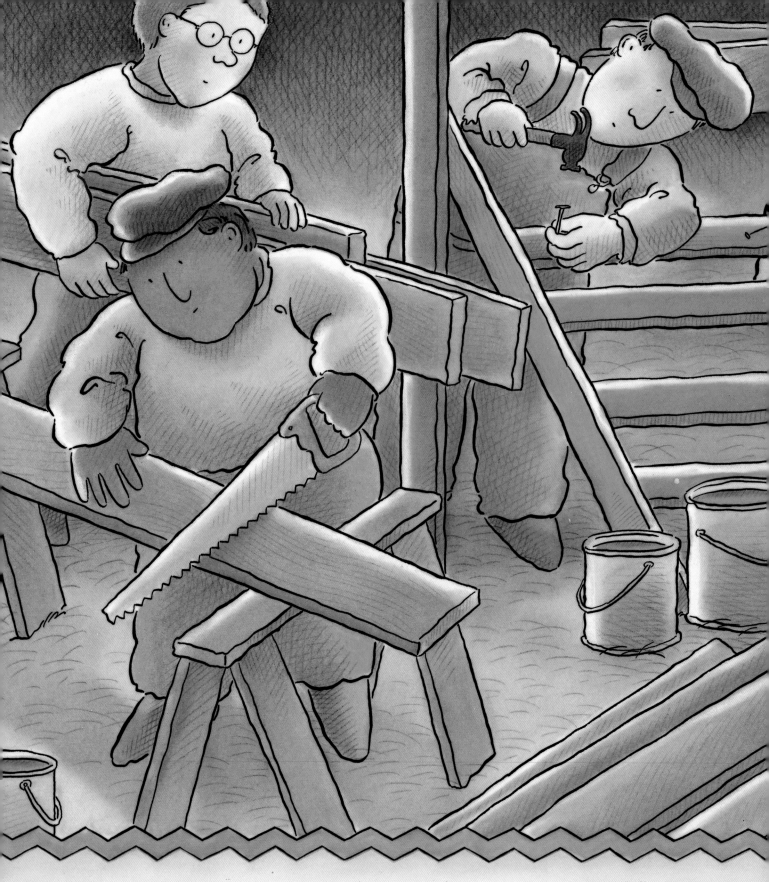

Ginger did not give up hope. Every day she practiced her act and every night she performed. In between, as the audience took its seats, Ginger stood watch, certain her little girl would appear.

At practice one day, Sir Deedrick had news. "Three new clowns are joining our circus," he said. "The Kellys need a very hardworking dog for their act." Ginger saw a smug grin creep across Prunella's dog lips. "Ginger," Sir Deedrick went on, "I have picked you. Tomorrow I will begin teaching you a

jump with these stairs and the trampoline. By the time the clowns arrive, you'll be perfect."

"What! That fumbler?" Prunella snapped.

Ginger looked things over.

The stairs were low and the trampoline soft and bouncy. Even a cat could do it, Ginger thought, chuckling to herself. And maybe, being in the spotlight, *she* would be noticed by her little girl. Yes . . . she was ready.

But the next morning, Ginger was not so sure. Now that it was all built, the staircase looked impossibly high and the trampoline impossibly low.

"Don't worry," Sir Deedrick said, "we'll begin on an easy step."

Over and over Ginger practiced jumping from a low stair to the trampoline and bouncing out into Sir Deedrick's arms.

"Good, Ginger," he said at last. "Now that you know how to jump safely, it's time for you to try it from the top."

Ginger climbed the stairs very slowly, her heart pounding. At the top she peeked over the edge of the platform. Sir Deedrick seemed tiny, far below.

"Ginger," he called, holding out his arms, "jump."

Ginger stepped closer to the edge, but then stopped. No matter how hard she tried, Ginger could not jump.

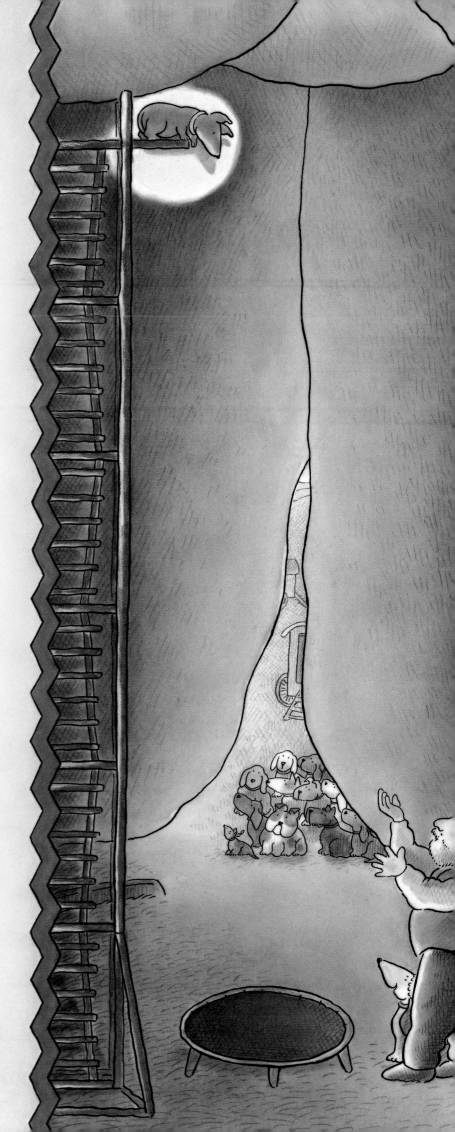

After a long wait, Sir Deedrick sighed. "It's okay, Ginger. You don't have to jump." Then he turned to the dog next to him. "Prunella, you give it a try."

Tail low, Ginger sadly walked down the stairs. She'd disappointed Sir Deedrick, and now her little girl would never find her.

Prunella pranced by on her way to the top. "I'm the only star of this show," she said, smirking. "No mutt will ever take my place."

Discouraged, Ginger watched as Prunella flawlessly jumped onto the trampoline and sailed into Sir Deedrick's arms.

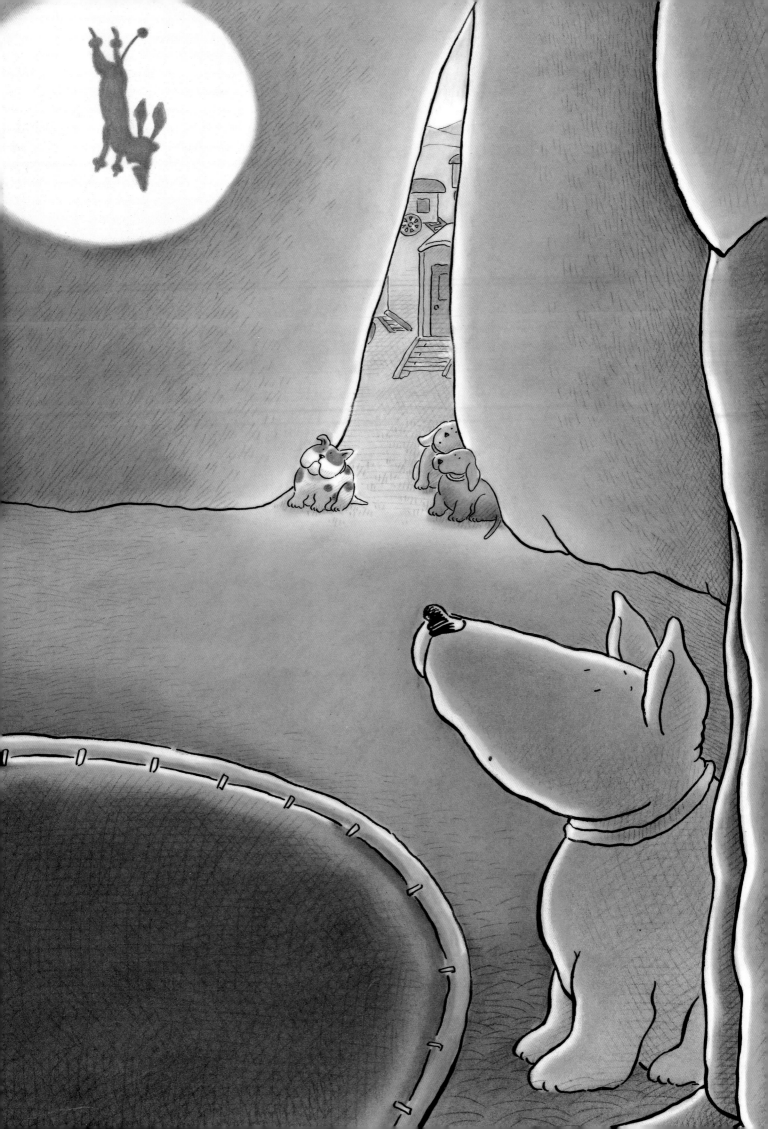

The next morning, Sir Dee-drick announced that Prunella would be performing with the new clowns and would be moving to live in their circus wagon. Ginger would do her usual tricks with the other dogs.

On the day the new clowns were to arrive, Ginger watched as Prunella showed off the grand bow she planned to make that evening. "I am the great Prunella," she sang, "Princess of the Big Top."

Now doubts filled Ginger's mind. Weary of searching, she began to wonder if she would be alone forever. That night, while Sir Deedrick readied the dogs for their show, Ginger hardly noticed the hubbub. "Maybe my little girl is just a dream," she said.

In the opening parade, the dazzling circus troop circled the ring. There were dancers in beautiful costumes, acrobats, and animal trainers. There were elephants, lions, horses, and of course, Sir Deedrick with his dogs.

The spotlight in the center shone on the ringmaster. *"Lai-dies and gen-tle-*

men!" he boomed. "Welcome to the most spectacular show in the world!"

Trumpets blared, lights flashed. The circus had begun! Then, as the parade filed out, the ringmaster signaled for the staircase and trampoline to be moved into place.

"Now," the ringmaster roared, "those Clowning Kellys and that Precious Poodle of Precision, Prunella!" The drum roll began.

Ginger watched the three clowns and Prunella step out of the shadows and bow. Excited by the applause, Prunella grandly swept her forepaws from side to side and twirled about. But then something happened. Was it a pebble under her toe? A gnat in her ear? Whatever, Prunella stumbled and fell flat on her face.

The drum roll stopped; the clapping stopped. In the great silence, Prunella looked up with a glare.

Suddenly, the night air was filled with a single magical laugh. Ginger felt tingly all over. She *knew* that sound — it was her little girl's laugh. And it had come from the smallest new clown.

Ginger was stunned. She had been searching for so long ... and now this. She had to think fast. Soon Prunella would be climbing those stairs and jumping, maybe right into the arms of her little girl. And then, a worse thought: Prunella would go to live with the clowns. With her family. It was too much.

By now, Prunella was back on her feet. Dashing for the steps, Ginger knocked her aside. The audience laughed and whistled at the foolishness. What a show!

Laughter grew to shouts as Ginger raced higher and higher. The drum roll started up again.

Nearing the top, Ginger took each step carefully, trying to remember everything Sir Deedrick had taught her. At the edge of the platform, Ginger stepped back. There, spread out below her, was the circus. Hundreds of expectant faces looked up, waiting. But then she saw Sir Deedrick on the far side of the ring. "You can do it, Ginger," he called up.

She looked at the three clowns: a *family*. They stood in position, ready to catch her.

The air grew hushed as the small clown stepped forward. "Ginger," she sang, "jump!"

And, taking a deep breath, Ginger jumped.

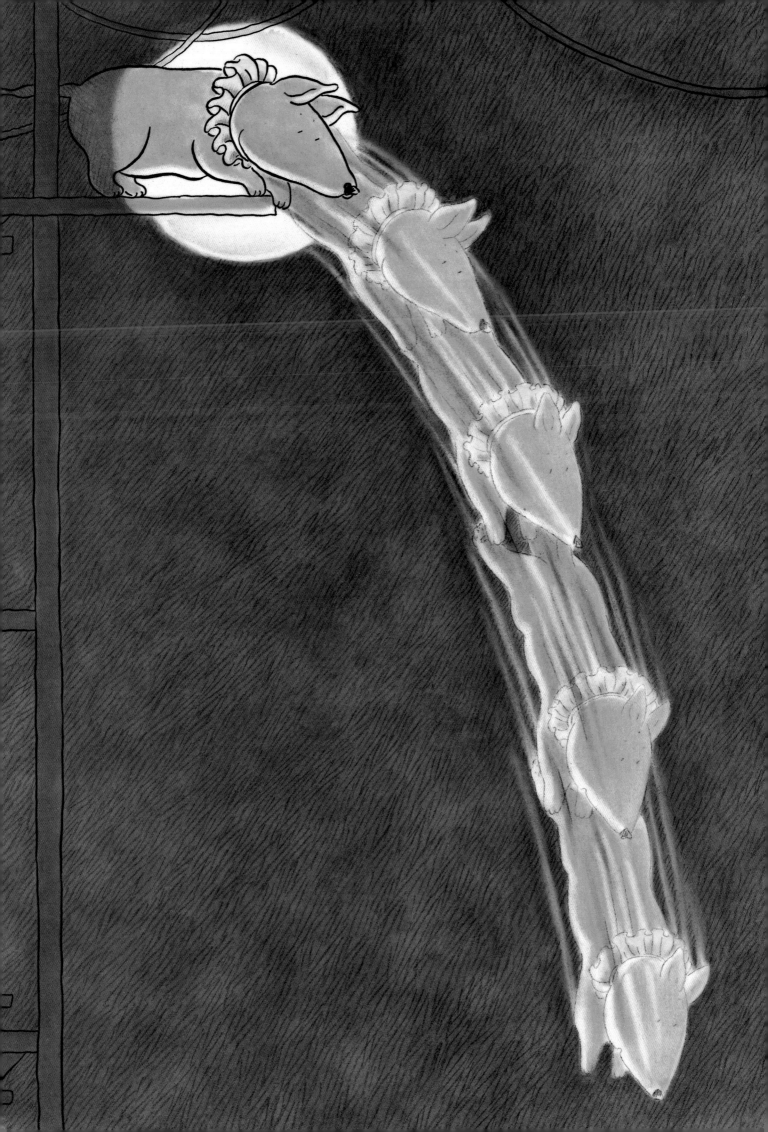

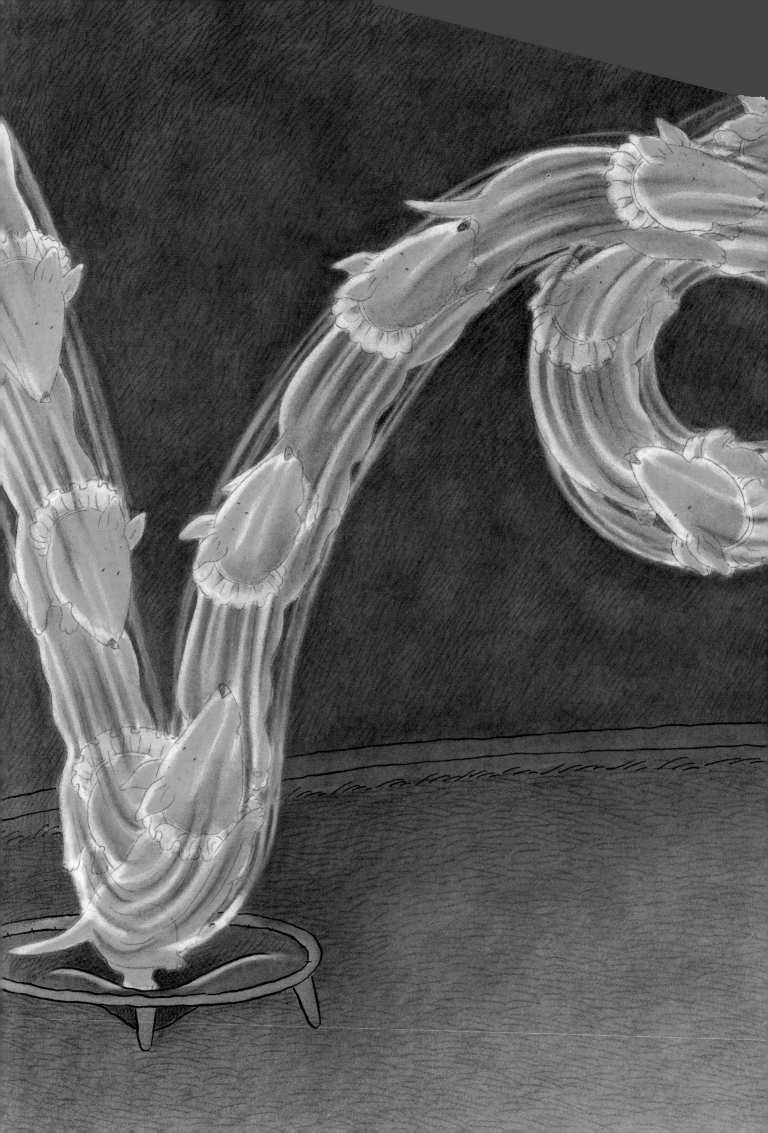

Wooomf! Ginger landed in the little clown's arms, sending them both tumbling back against the two tall clowns.

The crowd went wild. They cheered and threw popcorn in the air like confetti. Such a jump!

But to Ginger the applause was only a distant sound. Her ears were filled with the clown's laugh, and then a whisper as the little girl leaned close: "Don't be scared anymore. We'll be home soon."

A family! This was better than any dream. "I knew I would find you," Ginger wanted to whisper back, but instead she lay her head on the clown's shoulder, and laughed a dog laugh that only the little girl could hear.